The Moon in the Sky

Poems your kids would have written (if only they could write)

Written by Bruce Shutts
Illustrated by Amy Wummer

The Moon in the Sky: Poems Your Kids Would Have Written (If Only They Could Write)
Published by Stinson Books
Plymouth, MA

Publisher's Cataloging-in-Publication data

Names: Shutts, Bruce, author. | Wummer, Amy, illustrator.
Title: The moon in the sky : poems your kids would have written (if only they could write) / Bruce Shutts ; illustrated by Amy Wummer.
Description: Plymouth, MA: Stinson Books, 2022. | Summary: Thirteen whimsical poems that capture the simple honesty of everyday childhood activities written from a 3—6-year-olds perspective. From getting dressed, eating snacks or having stinky feet, you and your child will recognize yourself in these poems.
Identifiers: ISBN: 978-1-7376349-1-1 (hardcover) | 978-1-7376349-0-4 (paperback)
Subjects: LCSH Poetry, collections. | Children's poetry, American. | BISAC JUVENILE FICTION / Poetry
Classification: LCC PZ7.1.S5184 Moo 2021 | DDC 811.6--dc23

ISBN: 978-1-7376349-0-4

JUVENILE FICTION / Poetry

Interior layout by Victoria Wolf, wolfdesignandmarketing.com, copyright owned by Bruce P. Shutts.

Illustrations and cover by Amy Wummer

QUANTITY PURCHASES: Schools, companies, professional groups, clubs, and other organizations may qualify for special terms when ordering quantities of this title. For information, email bps44@comcast.net

...to all the Nanas

Getting Dressed

My mommy used to dress me
When I was very small.
But now I do it by myself,
And it's not hard at all!
My pants are really easy,
Since both my feet will fit.
And after I put both legs in,
I pull them up. That's it!
But shirts are very tricky;

They have three holes, not two!
And if you pick the wrong one,
Your head just won't go through!
My shoes can go on easily,
But sometimes they're too tight.
My mom says that's because I need
To know my left and right.
And soon I am all finished;
A minute's all it took.
So now I'll ask my mommy
To tell me how I look!

A Bug in the Bathroom

I sat down on the toilet,
Because I had to pee.
Then looked up at the ceiling
To see what I could see.
That's when I saw a great big bug
Come crawling down the wall.
But I am not afraid of bugs!
I didn't mind at all!
His legs were long and skinny;
He crawled along real slow.
So I just kept on watching him,
To see where he would go!
"Now, if you want to stay up there,
Then you won't bother me."
But, "Mr. Bug, Please don't come down,
Because I have to pee!"

My Car Seat

I have a car seat just for me
And use it every day;
But first, I have to buckle up,
'Cause it's more safe that way.
A lot of times, we make one stop,
But sometimes three or four.
The one trip that we always take
Is to the grocery store.
But when we drive to Nana's house,
The ride is always long,
Then Daddy puts the music on
And we all sing along.
I try to never make a fuss,
And then I'll get a treat.

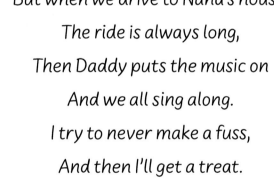

But once I wasn't careful
And spilled some on my seat!
I sit right by the window,
So I can look outside.
My car seat is the perfect place
To sit and take a ride!

 oys

I started using markers,
When I was very small.
And now I stay between the lines,
And NEVER on the wall!

I like to use my building blocks,
And see how high they'll get.
But when my sister knocks them down,
I really get upset!

My toys are sometimes fun to share
When I am with a friend,
But if I'm playing by myself,
Then I will just pretend!
Now some toys run on batteries,

Which makes them go real fast;
But don't forget to turn them off,
Since batteries won't last!
And when I'm done with all my toys,
My mom says what to do.
She tells me cleaning up is fun.
But I don't think that's true!

Boo-Boos

I bet you've had a boo-boo;
You're not the only one.
Now I've had lots of boo-boos,

And they are not much fun.
When I am crawling on the floor
Or jumping on the bed,
I don't watch where I'm going,
And then I bump my head!
Or when I'm outside running,

I'll trip and scrape my knee,
Or maybe pinch my finger,
Now THAT sure bothers me.
So when your boo-boo really hurts,
Please try not to be sad.
Your mom will put a Band-Aid on,
And soon it won't be bad.

Snacks

When Mom says I can have a snack,
Trust me, that's good news.
But sometimes it's a problem when
I don't know what to choose!
Crackers are my favorite,
Especially with cheese,

But what I love is yogurt
In a tube that I can squeeze.
Fruit is always fun to eat,
And doesn't fill me up.
My mommy always slices them,

Then puts them in a cup.
Now often I won't get to eat
Exactly what I pick.
Like once I asked for M&Ms,
And got a carrot stick!
There are so many types of snacks,
And all are fun to munch.
But just because you have a snack
You still must eat your lunch!

Picking My Nose

While I was watching some TV, my nose began to itch.

I gave it just a wiggle and then a little twitch.

I moved my finger up in there, an inch or so, I'd say.

But when my mommy looked at me, I turned the other way!

I had to do some poking, and then I pulled it out.

"THAT'S SO GROSS," my mommy said, as loud as she could shout!

I should have used a tissue or napkin, I suppose.

But what if you don't have one?

You HAVE to pick your nose!

I Have a Baby Sister

I have a baby sister
I'd like to talk about.
She was in Mommy's tummy till
The doctor took her out!
I moved into another room,
So she could stay with us.
She sure does like to sleep a lot,
And sometimes makes a fuss!
I try to make a funny face,
To see if she will smile.

I wish that she would talk to me,
  But that might take a while!
I watch when Mommy feeds her,
  Before she takes a nap.
And if I'm very careful,
  I'll hold her on my lap!
I hope that she will grow up soon,
  And I can hardly wait!
For then the two of us can play.
  And wouldn't that be great?

Taking a Walk

Of all the things that you can do

When it's a sunny day,

"Who wants to go out for a walk?"

Is what my mom would say.

Now sometimes if I'm tired

Or want to stay inside,

She pops me in the stroller

And takes me for a ride.

I always like to play "I Spy"

As we go down the street.

And once I saw a doggy,

Who had to sniff my feet!

But if I want to walk myself,
My mom says I can try.
We never seem to go as fast,
And I'm not sure just why!
It doesn't really matter

If I walk or skip or run.
The one thing that I know for sure,
That taking walks is fun!

Mac and Cheese

Hooray hooray for mac and cheese,

It's what I love to eat.

When Mom and Dad eat other stuff,

I get to have this treat!

Now, if I try it with a fork,

A lot falls on the floor.

But if I try it with a spoon,

Then I can pick up more!

And when my bowl is empty,

I ask my mommy, "Please,"
"May I just have another scoop?"
Hooray for mac and cheese!

Stinky Feet

In summer, when the weather's warm,
And I go out to play,
My mom says I don't need my socks;
My feet stay cool that way.

I run around and play all day
And hardly take a rest,
Until it's time to come inside
And start to get undressed.
My sneaks come off, and that's OK,

As far as I can tell,
Till Mom and Daddy look at me
And ask me, "What's that smell?"
I tell my dad to smell my feet,
To see what he will do.
He gets real close to take a sniff,
And then he yells, "PEE-EW!"

He says I have some smelly bears,
And that just makes me laugh.
I guess that it can only mean
It's time to take my bath!

Bath Time

First, I take off all my clothes
And throw them to and fro.
I grab my toys and bubble bath
And in the tub, I go.
I can't turn on the water yet,
Because I'm not that old.
Only Dad can get it right,
And not too hot or cold!

I'm not supposed to splash too much,
But sometimes I forget.
And Daddy doesn't seem to mind
When he gets soaking wet!
After I have played a while,
The next thing that I do
Is wash my hair all by myself

With special kids' shampoo,
And when it's time to rinse it,
I really am quite wise.
I learned that it won't sting at all,
If you just close your eyes!

How Come?

How come I have to go to bed,
When I just want to play?
How come I have to clean my room?
I did it yesterday!
How come I can't do all the things
That older kids can do?
How come I have to take just one,
When really I want two!?
How come when I talk super loud,
My mom will whisper "Quiet?"
How come when I won't take a bite,

She'll ask me just to "Try it."
How come I have to wear a hat,
When I don't think it's cold?
How come that I can't go to school
Till I am five years old?
I guess I'll have to do the things
That Mom and Dad both say.
And I won't ask "How come" again;
(At least no more today!)

About the Title

This book was inspired by a poem, "The Moon in the Sky," written around 1960 by my wife Linda (a Nana) and her mother (also a Nana) as a second-grade school assignment. It has been passed down through three generations.

The Moon in the Sky

The moon in the sky,
Shines so bright.
It looks to me
Like an electric light!
But lights burn out
And break in two,
While this old man
Stays good as new!

—Nana and Nana

Acknowledgments

"The Moon in the Sky" would not exist without the incredible illustrative work provided by Amy Wummer. I want to thank her for her patience in working with me, a first-time author, and for her creative input. Next, I want to thank the folks at My Word Publishing, especially Amanda Miller, who guided me through the self-publishing maze, and Polly Letofsky, for her expertise in book marketing. I want to thank Victoria Wolf for her skillful interior design of this book. Finally, Delta Donohue for the proof editing necessary for someone who never learned correct punctuation!

By all means, I want to thank my three children, Megan, Amanda, and Jeffrey, for providing me with all of those precious moments which I have tried to re-create in this book and for their wise advice to make sure that *"I got it right!"* In advance, I also want to thank my grandchildren Conor, Elliott, Sadie, Camden, and Teddy, who will surely provide me with the ultimate feedback when we sit down to read *"The Moon in the Sky."*

Finally, I want to thank my lovely wife, Linda, who started this journey with her original version of *"The Moon in the Sky"* at age eight, along with her mother, Virginia. For the past fifty-two years, she has been the recipient of many of my silly poems and has helped me create many others. Not only has she been my number one fan but also my best friend in the whole world!

About the Author

Bruce Shutts has spent countless hours reading children's picture books to his three children and five grandchildren over the past forty years. He also loves to create humorous poems for nearly every occasion he can imagine. Coupled with the fact that he often thinks and acts like a three-to-six-year-old, it makes his entrance into the world of children's

books a natural fit. He currently is retired with his wife of forty-five years and loves to travel, play golf, and (you guessed it) read books at night to his grandkids!

About the Illustrator

Amy Wummer has been working in the field of illustration since the early nineties. She is known primarily as a children's book illustrator, with more than 150 titles to her credit. Amy specializes in whimsical, lighthearted themes and works in pencil, ink, and watercolors. She is the recipient of numerous awards for her illustrations. She and her husband, Mark, also a artist, live in Pennsylvania. They are the parents of three grow children. Besides drawing and painting (of course!), Amy loves to cook, sew, read, visit new places, and do fun things with her family, especially her six grandchildren!

Made in the USA
Columbia, SC
16 February 2022

55918248R00020